RAIN OR SHINE

Adapted by Tracey West
Illustrated by Jay Johnson

ISBN 0-439-80350-0
Copyright © 2006 Scholastic Entertainment Inc. All rights reserved. SCHOLASTIC, MAYA & MIGUEL and logos are trademarks of Scholastic Inc.
12 11 10 9 8 7 6 5 4 3 2   6 7 8 9 10/0
Printed in the U.S.A.
First printing, June 2006

SCHOLASTIC INC.

New York   Toronto   London   Auckland   Sydney
Mexico City   New Delhi   Hong Kong   Buenos Aires

"Earth Day is next week," Mrs. Langley told Maya and Miguel's class. "Each one of you needs to work on a project. You can work alone, or in teams."

Maya was so excited.

"I loooooove Earth Day!" she said. "It's all about taking care of the earth so there will be fresh air and clean water and . . ."

The school bell rang, but Maya kept talking.

"Did I say that I looooooove Earth Day?"

On the way home from school, Maya, Miguel, and their friends tried to think of an Earth Day project.

"What if we adopt a rain forest animal?" Chrissy asked.

"Or we could make a worm farm," Miguel said.

The friends walked by an empty lot.

"When did this place get so full of trash and stuff?" Andy asked.

"*¡Eso es!*" Maya cried as her ponytail bobbles lit up. "I have an idea!"

"We should clean up the lot for our Earth Day project," Maya said.

Maya imagined that she and her friends had super powers. They would clean up cans, pile up newspapers, and say good-bye to garbage!

The next day at school, Mrs. Langley had exciting news. "The Global Earth Day Committee is going to visit our school," she said. "They will select one project for their website. Your project could be seen by people around the world!"

Maya was worried. What if their project was not good enough to win?

She quickly raised her hand. "I forgot to say one thing. After we clean the lot, we are going to plant a community garden!"

"I just looooooove Earth Day!" Maya said.
But her friends were not so excited.
"We don't know how to plant a garden,"
Andy pointed out.

"No problem," Maya said. "I found this on the Internet. It tells us everything we need to know about planting a garden," she said. "Isn't that great?"
Everyone groaned.

Maya, Miguel, and their friends worked on their garden plans.
Tito had another idea.

He watched a man buy something from the Santos'
Pet Store. The man threw his plastic bag in a trash can.
Then the wind blew it away. . . .

Tito talked to Gus, owner of the bakery.
"Why do you use paper bags?" he asked.
"Paper bags are better for the environment," Gus said.
"But the best thing to do is bring your own bag from
home, and re-use it."

"In the United States we use over 300 billion plastic bags a year," Gus added. "That is a waste of resources."

Tito thought about this. "Thanks, Gus. You gave me a good idea!"

Maya and the others started cleaning up the lot.
"Okay, Earth Day team members," Maya said.
"Let's move out!"

Maya tried moving some old tires. She got stuck inside of one. She rolled and rolled . . . right into some cans Andy was recycling!

It was hard work. But nobody gave up.

The kids finally finished cleaning the lot. But there were piles of heavy junk left.

"This all needs to go to the recycling center," Chrissy said. "We need some help."

Miguel shook his head. "I knew we should have done the worm farm."

Then Maya saw Gus's bakery truck. "*¡Eso es!*" she cried.

Maya talked to Gus. He agreed to drive the junk to the recycling center.

"The lot looks great!" Gus said. "Good job!"

Mrs. Langley talked to the class the next day.

"There is a change of plans," she said. "The Global Earth Day Committee will be coming to look at your projects this afternoon."

"But I thought it was tomorrow!" Maya blurted out.

The kids walked back to the empty lot.

"We will never plant a whole garden in just a few hours," Maggie said.

"Never say never, Maggie," Maya told her. "We just have to take things one step at a time."

Everyone got to work.

First, they got rid of the rocks and weeds. Then they turned the soil to get it ready for planting. They got a lot done. Even Paco helped!

Tito was busy, too.

He got Mr. Santos to switch to paper bags at the pet store.

He got other people to bring their own bags from home.

Back at the garden, the kids were ready to plant. "Nothing can stop us from winning that prize!" Maya cried. "Nothing!"

And then it started to rain. . . .

"Come on, guys!" Maya cheered. "Where's your Earth Day spirit?"

"I guess it's stuck in the mud," Theo said.

Everyone walked away from the lot—even Miguel.

But Maya didn't give up. She tried to plant a tree in the muddy ground. She dragged the heavy tree across the lot. Then she slipped and fell!

Maya felt a hand reach out to help her. It was Miguel!
"I guess I just loooooove Earth Day!" Miguel said.
"We want to help, too, Maya," Chrissy said.
Maya turned around. All of her friends had come back!

The rain poured down. But everyone kept working.
Soon they were all covered in mud!

Mrs. Langley brought the Earth Day committee to see their project.

"Welcome to our community garden," Miguel said.

The judges looked at the muddy lot. Maya smiled. "It's a work in progress," she said.

Back at the school cafeteria, the committee took photos of Tito.

"The committee has chosen Tito," Mrs. Langley explained. "He convinced people in the neighborhood to stop using plastic bags."

"Congratulations, Tito!" Maya said. "Would you help us finish our garden this weekend?"

"Earth Day is today, though," Mrs. Langley said.

"But we should celebrate it every day, right?" Maya asked.

"Can I just add one more thing?" Maya asked.
"We know, Maya," Miguel said. "We love Earth Day, too!"